THE AMULET
OF AVANTIA

NixA
THE
DEATH-BRINGER

With special thanks to Cherith Baldry

For Miroslav Torak, with all good wishes

www.beastquest.co.uk

ORCHARD BOOKS
338 Euston Road, London NW1 3BH
Orchard Books Australia
Level 17/207 Kent St, Sydney, NSW 2000

A Paperback Original
First published in Great Britain in 2009

Beast Quest is a registered trademark of Beast Quest Limited
Series created by Beast Quest Limited, London

Text © Beast Quest Limited 2009
Cover and inside illustrations by Steve Sims © Beast Quest Limited 2009

A CIP catalogue record for this book is available from
the British Library.

ISBN 978 1 40830 376 4

15

Printed and bound by CPI Group (UK) Ltd, Croydon, CR0 4YY

The paper and board used in this paperback are natural recyclable
products made from wood grown in sustainable forests. The
manufacturing processes conform to the environmental regulations of
the country of origin.

Orchard Books is a division of Hachette Children's Books,
an Hachette UK company

www.hachette.co.uk

NixA
THE
DEATH-BRINGER

BY ADAM BLADE

ORCHARD

The Forbidden Land

THE DEAD VALLEY

THE DEAD JUNGLE

THE DARK WOOD

THE DEAD PEAKS

All hail, fellow followers of the Quest.

We have not met before, but like you, I have been watching Tom's adventures with a close eye. Do you know who I am? Have you heard of Taladon the Swift, Master of the Beasts? I have returned – just in time for my son, Tom, to save me from a fate worse than death. The evil wizard, Malvel, has stolen something precious from me, and until Tom is able to complete another Quest, I cannot be returned to full life. I must wait between worlds, neither human nor ghost. I am half the man I once was and only Tom can return me to my former glory.

Will Tom have the strength of heart to help his father? This new Quest would test even the most determined hero. And there may be a heavy price for my son to pay if he defeats six more Beasts...

All I can do is hope – that Tom is successful and that I will one day be returned to full strength. Will you put your power behind Tom and wish him well? I know I can count on my son – can I count on you, too? Not a moment can be wasted. As this latest Quest unfolds, much rides upon it.

We must all be brave.

Taladon

PROLOGUE

Farmer Gretlin stood at the edge of
his wheat field. Two days ago, the
wheat had been waist high, shining
golden in the sun. Now it was dull
grey, almost black, and a damp,
musty smell came from it.

"This is worse than when the
crops were scorched by fire," Gretlin
muttered to himself. "Is Errinel under
threat again?"

The farmer strode out into the

wheat field, pushing aside the dying stems. He was desperately searching for any patches that were as yet untouched by this evil blight. At the opposite side of the field the wheat was still golden, but most of his crop had been destroyed.

The harsh rays of the morning sun slanted down, dazzling Gretlin as they struck something on the ground. Shielding his eyes, the farmer saw a tiny, strange metallic object half-buried in the earth.

As he reached to pick it up, the wheat rustled around him, though there was no wind. The stalks curved and swooped, like dozens of arms trying to hold him back.

Confused, Gretlin backed away from the metal object. The wheat hissed and thrashed around him. "It's alive!" he whispered, turning to flee.

He pushed his way through the writhing stalks of wheat to the edge of the field, then halted as he heard a voice carried on the breeze. He pressed his hands to his ears – the sound stung like his eardrums had been slashed with razors.

Looking to see where the voice was coming from, Gretlin spotted a woman at the opposite side of the wheat field, where the crop still grew tall and strong. She was slender, with long golden hair; she wore robes of scarlet silk that floated out around her as she walked towards the farmer. She cast handfuls of glittering dust over the wheat, and where it fell the golden stalks shrivelled and turned grey. Around her feet were the still bodies of other villagers, slumped on the ground.

"Hey!" Gretlin shouted. "Stop that!" Angrily he began to run towards the woman, waving his arms above his head. "Get away from my wheat!"

The woman glided up to him, her bare feet hardly touching the ground. She held out her hand. A strange silver object with a sliver of blue enamel rested on her open palm. It looked like the thing Gretlin had seen half-buried in the earth.

Squinting in the sunlight, he

realised that it was a piece broken off a much larger object. He could just make out faintly etched marks on one side. Then his mouth gaped in astonishment as he realised that the scrap of metal wasn't resting on the woman's hand – it was floating just above it!

"Who are you?" Gretlin asked, his voice hoarse with fear. Surely she couldn't be human!

"My name is Nixa." Now the woman's voice was soft and beautiful.

But as she spoke the bright morning sky changed to a threatening purple. Clouds swallowed up the sun. The purple darkened to black.

"What's happening?" Gretlin gasped.

The air vibrated with a sound like thunder. As the farmer stared in horror, the woman began to change.

Her arms split and became a mass of thrashing tentacles. Her two eyes divided into a cluster of bulging, glistening spheres. Her scarlet robes dissolved and her body sagged into a thousand wrinkles. Green slime seeped out from her and dripped onto the ground. Gretlin choked on the foul stench that flooded around him.

"My name is Nixa," the monster repeated. Her voice still sounded like a beautiful chime of bells, but it stabbed Gretlin's ears like a knife. He clapped his hands to the sides of his head and felt blood spurting between his fingers.

Farmer Gretlin screamed as a mass of tentacles reached out towards him.

CHAPTER ONE

A FATHER RETURNS

"One hundred and fifty-one! One hundred and fifty-two!" Captain Harkman's voice echoed across the training courtyard.

Tom groaned as he pumped his arms in yet another press-up. He thought he was going to die of boredom, if he didn't first melt into a puddle under the hot sun of Avantia.

He remembered how he had returned from Gorgonia a few weeks before, fresh from the Quest where he had defeated the evil wizard, Malvel, for the third time.

"Avantia owes you a great debt," King Hugo had said. "Tom, you may choose any position you like in my court. Ask, and it's yours."

"Thank you, sire," Tom had replied. "I'd like to be a soldier in your army."

He'd thought it would be fun, and a great way to go on helping Avantia. "But I was wrong," he sighed to himself. What was the point of doing press-ups all day long when he had powers that the cadet officer, Captain Harkman, had never dreamt of?

"I made a mistake," Tom muttered to himself as his arms pumped up and down. "I wish there was something else I could do. Maybe another Quest…"

He snatched a glance across the courtyard to where his friend, Elenna, was teaching archery to the youngest cadets. He watched her positioning one boy's fingers on the bowstring, and saw his face break into a delighted grin as his arrow thumped home.

Tom heard heavy footsteps. Captain Harkman's feet halted beside him; he was tapping his whip against his polished riding boots.

"Slacking again?" Captain Harkman snarled. He crouched down beside Tom, so that Tom could see his red, sweating face and gingery hair. "You're just like your father. He was a slacker, too."

Fury flooded through Tom. He gritted his teeth together with the

effort of controlling his temper.

"Taladon trained here once, when
he was a young man," the Captain
went on, straightening up. "I was
glad to see the back of him. He was
lazy and arrogant. He was—"

Tom heard the sound of an arrow
whizzing through the air. It just
missed Captain Harkman's head as
he ducked and rolled away.

"Who fired that?" he yelled, bouncing to his feet again.

Elenna ran over, bow in hand, and halted in front of the Captain.

"Sorry," she said. "It was one of my cadets. He hasn't quite got the hang of archery yet."

Tom hid a smile. He knew perfectly well that Elenna had fired the arrow herself. Just because they weren't on a Beast Quest didn't mean that he and Elenna wouldn't watch each other's backs anymore.

A voice called out from the palace gardens. "He has returned! Taladon the Swift has returned!"

Tom froze. *Taladon? My father?*

Breathlessly, he scrambled to his feet and pounded towards the archway that separated the training courtyard from the gardens, weaving his way between his fellow cadets.

"Hey! You there! Come back!"

Tom ignored Captain Harkman's shouts. He didn't care how the Captain would punish him, if only he could see his father.

He heard light footsteps racing behind. He knew who that would be – Elenna.

Bursting through the archway, Tom saw one of the King's messengers dashing across the gardens. "He's here!" he yelled. "Taladon has returned!"

Tom took the steps up to the main palace door three at a time. The guards by the open doors waved him through and he ran down the long corridor that led towards King Hugo's throne room.

My father left when I was a baby,

he thought. *Am I really going to see him now?*

Dashing around a corner, Tom came to a halt. The throne-room doors were open and a man was stepping through them. The sun slanting through a nearby window outlined his broad shoulders and long, black cloak. He strode forwards confidently, his head held high.

"Father!" Tom sprang towards him, but the man didn't seem to have heard. He walked on without looking back, and the guards pulled the throne-room doors closed behind him.

"Father?" Tom repeated to himself, as he stood alone in the corridor.

CHAPTER TWO

MAN OR GHOST?

"Was that Taladon?" Elenna panted, as she caught up with Tom outside the throne room.

"I...I'm not sure." Tom's heart was thumping hard at the glimpse of the tall man.

"There's only one way to find out," Elenna said, nodding at the closed doors of the throne room.

The guards pushed the doors open

again and Tom hurried forwards with Elenna at his side.

Inside, King Hugo sat on his throne with the good wizard of Avantia, Aduro, standing beside him. But they didn't look as happy as Tom had expected. The wizard's face was pale, and King Hugo's eyes were wide with shock; his hands gripped the arms of his throne so hard that his knuckles were white. The King's courtiers stood around, whispering uneasily.

Sudden fear seized Tom. He stumbled to a halt. The figure he had seen in the corridor was kneeling in front of King Hugo. "Father?" Tom asked.

The man rose to his feet and turned. He was tall with a thatch of dark hair, a curling brown beard, and deep-set brown eyes. He wore a travel-stained tunic and leggings, covered by a dusty black cloak.

"I can see he's your father," Elenna whispered. "He looks just like you will when you're grown up."

The man looked at Tom and held his gaze; Tom could not look away. He waited for the flood of emotions, but...nothing happened. *Shouldn't I be glad to see my father?* he thought. Somehow this wasn't how he had imagined their first meeting.

Taladon smiled. "My son," he said. His voice sounded rusty, as if he hadn't used it in a long time.

Elenna nudged Tom. "Go on!"

Dazed, Tom stumbled forwards to give his father a hug. But when he tried to wrap his arms around Taladon, they passed right through him, as if his father were no more solid than a wisp of cloud.

A gasp came from the King's courtiers and Tom heard Elenna stifle a cry. Wizard Aduro whispered something to King Hugo, and the King waved a hand at his followers. "Leave us," he ordered. "Everyone except Aduro, Tom and Elenna."

As the courtiers and the guards filed out, glancing nervously at Tom and his father, Tom stepped back. Icy shivers were running through his body. Taladon was looking down at him, his eyes filled with love and sadness.

"What's happened?" Tom gasped. "Are you a ghost? Are you *dead*?"

Aduro crossed the throne room to shut the doors on the last of the courtiers. Returning to the King's side, he stopped beside Taladon. He

raised one hand; a glittering mist
flowed from his fingers and wrapped
Taladon in its silver coils. Then it
returned to Wizard Aduro and
vanished.

Aduro bent his head as if he were listening. "Taladon lives," he said at last, "but he is stranded between the real world and the spirit world. Taladon, has this anything to do with the Ghost Beasts?"

Taladon nodded.

"Ghost Beasts?" Tom felt more confused than ever. "What are *they*? I've never heard of them."

"Sit down, Tom." Taladon pointed to a footstool at the bottom of the steps leading to the throne. "Aduro and I will tell you everything."

Tom went to the footstool and sat down. Elenna fetched a second stool and sat next to him. Tom was glad she was there.

Wizard Aduro swept his wand through the air. White fire flared out of it and formed a glowing circle in the middle of the throne room.

"Keep your eyes on that," Aduro instructed Tom and Elenna. "It will show you what has happened to Taladon."

"And the Ghost Beasts?" Elenna asked. "I thought we destroyed all the Beasts in Gorgonia."

"Malvel's most deadly Beasts have yet to be revealed to you. And they don't live in Gorgonia," Wizard Aduro told her solemnly. "They are here, in the darkest corners of Avantia."

"*Here?*" Tom exclaimed, his stomach churning.

King Hugo nodded, his eyes troubled. "I had hoped that they would never rise to trouble Avantia again," he murmured. "That's why we didn't tell you about them, Tom."

"The Ghost Beasts live in the Forbidden Land," Aduro went on.

Tom and Elenna exchanged a startled glance.

"What's the Forbidden Land?" Elenna asked. "I've never heard of such a place."

"Few people in Avantia know of it," Aduro told her. "A wall surrounds

it to keep them out. It is dangerous to set foot there."

"Because of the Ghost Beasts?" Tom said.

"Yes," the wizard told him. "They thrive on its shadows and gloom. No normal man can touch them, and they are able to cause the worst destruction imaginable. In their ghostly form they take risks that even a normal Beast would think twice about." His voice grew harder and his eyes flashed. "Tom,
I hope you can be brave. These are the most dangerous Beasts ever!"

CHAPTER THREE

A NEW QUEST

Tom felt a spark of excitement. Was this the beginning of a new Quest?

Taladon stretched out a hand towards the magical screen. The silver fire died, and Tom saw a picture of a rocky hillside. An armoured knight was there, his sword in his hand. Tom recognised the golden armour that belonged to the Master of the Beasts.

The knight raised his sword high above his head, ready to bring it down on a beautiful, golden-haired woman dressed in scarlet robes.

"Is that you?" Tom asked his father, growing confused. "Fighting someone who isn't even armed?"

"Watch," Taladon said.

The knight brought his sword whistling down, but it passed right through the woman's body, just as Tom's arms had passed through Taladon. At the same moment the woman began to change. Her arms sprouted into tentacles, and her beautiful face became hideously wrinkled, with a cluster of staring, evil eyes.

Elenna drew in her breath sharply. "Is that a Ghost Beast?"

Taladon nodded. "That is Nixa the

Death-Bringer. She is a deadly Beast who can take the shape of anything she wants. But her voice is always beautiful."

Tom shuddered. Somehow the idea of a beautiful voice made Nixa seem even more evil.

On the screen, Taladon and the woman battled together, the monster's tentacles wrapped round the armoured body of the knight.

"Was it Nixa who trapped you between life and death?" Tom asked.

Taladon shook his head. "Aduro armed me with the precious Amulet of Avantia," he replied.

"What's that?" Elenna's voice was filled with curiosity.

"It's a disc of blue and silver carved with powerful symbols," Aduro answered, stroking his beard. "I made it to protect the Master of the Beasts against the Ghost Beasts."

"And it served me well, until…" Taladon stretched out his arm and the picture of the battling knight and the monster faded. The magical screen darkened, as it was filled with swirling black cloud. Then the cloud cleared, and a familiar figure began to take shape. Tom recognised the black robes, the cruel features shadowed by a black hood, and the sunken eyes glittering with evil. A mocking laugh echoed through the darkness.

"Malvel!" Tom exclaimed, jumping to his feet as anger swelled inside him. "It was Malvel who trapped you!"

"It was." Taladon's eyes narrowed and his mouth set in a hard line; Tom could tell that his father shared his anger. "I defeated five of the six Ghost Beasts: Nixa the death-bringer, Equinus the spirit horse, Rashouk the cave troll, Luna the moon wolf and Blaze the ice dragon."

"What about the sixth?" Elenna asked. There was awe in her voice as she heard the names of the fearsome Beasts Taladon had conquered.

"The sixth was Stealth, the ghost panther." Taladon paced across the throne room, turned sharply, and pointed once more at the magical screen.

Tom sat down again to watch. The image of Malvel faded, to be replaced by a rocky hillside. On the topmost pinnacle a panther with three tails was perched. Its body was long and sleek. Its eyes were as green as jade.

As Tom stared in fascinated horror, the Ghost Beast leapt into the air, its muscular body blotting out the sky. It looked fiercer than any Beast Tom had ever faced.

"You fought *that*?" Tom breathed out, his gaze returning to his father. Taladon must be the bravest man in the world!

His father nodded. The picture on the screen blurred and formed again. Now Tom saw the Ghost Panther hovering over the crest of the hill, while Taladon, still wearing the golden armour, slashed his sword at its outstretched claws and ducked to avoid the Beast's snapping fangs. For the first time Tom noticed that his father wore a silver disc on a chain around his neck. There was a circle of bright blue in the centre of the disc.

The sky was split by a bolt of
black lightning. It struck Taladon in
the chest and he staggered back as the
silver amulet shattered into pieces and
spun away in glittering fragments.

Tom choked back a cry as he saw
Stealth swooping down on his father.
But the Beast's swiping paws passed
straight through Taladon's body.

"The lightning made you a ghost!"
Tom exclaimed.

"It was Malvel's lightning," Taladon replied. "After it struck me Malvel kept me a prisoner of his magic for a long time. Longer than I care to recall."

The magic screen showed Tom and Elenna a sphere of surging grey cloud, shot through with flashes of glittering black. Taladon, without his armour now, floated helplessly in the middle of it.

"What happened then?" Elenna asked.

Taladon gestured at the screen and the cloudy ball faded. His body drifted to the ground; he seemed to be in the middle of a flat plain under a threatening purple sky.

"That's Gorgonia!" Elenna said, glancing at Tom.

Taladon nodded. "Suddenly, I was

free. I started to walk across the plain, until I saw a shimmering archway leading into Avantia. I was able to escape from Malvel and come back here, and I still don't know why."

Aduro, who had been standing by the King's throne as he listened to the story, strode forwards again and thumped his staff on the floor. "That was the moment when Tom defeated Malvel for the third time," he explained. "Any magic, good or evil, grows weak if it has been repelled three times. Your son freed you, Taladon."

Taladon's gaze rested on Tom, his eyes warm with gratitude. "Thank you," he said quietly.

Tom's heart swelled with pride, but a moment later his anger surged back. He clenched his fists. "I'll make Malvel pay for what he's done to you!"

Looking puzzled, Taladon turned to Wizard Aduro. "I still don't understand *what* Malvel has done to me. Why am I a ghost?"

"And is he going to stay like this for ever?" Elenna added anxiously.

"The black lightning must have robbed you of your powers and trapped you between worlds," Aduro said thoughtfully. "But if the pieces of the amulet can be found and put back together, you will become the man you once were."

Tom and Elenna both leapt to their feet. "Then we have to find the pieces!" Tom exclaimed.

Wizard Aduro looked from Tom to Elenna and back again, a faint smile on his face. "You both have great courage," he said, "but it's not that simple. The amulet was broken into six pieces, and each is now guarded by a Ghost Beast. You can only restore Tom's father if you defeat all the Beasts and put the amulet together again as one. Remember, the Beasts will do everything in their power to keep the pieces from you, and may hide them if they have to. This Quest will be your biggest test yet."

Tom's stomach lurched as he thought of the two deadly Beasts he had seen on the magic screen, and remembered the others that Taladon had named. Even with his magical powers, could he hope to defeat all the evil creatures?

But Tom didn't hesitate. Saving Taladon was more important than anything. He hadn't waited this long for his father to return only to have him still so far away.

"This will be our next Quest," he said firmly.

Wizard Aduro and King Hugo exchanged a smile.

Elenna stood at Tom's shoulder, her eyes bright with determination. "Just tell us where we have to go," she said.

"Very well." Wizard Aduro inclined his head. "Avantia's two champions will leave first thing tomorrow morning."

Tom's whole body tingled with excitement. Taladon was back – in a way – and he had a new challenge.

This Quest will earn me the greatest prize I've ever won, he thought. *My father will be restored.*

CHAPTER FOUR

A BRUSH
WITH HOME

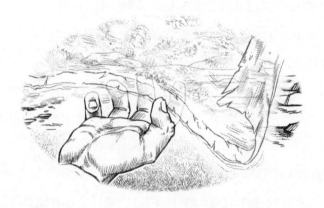

Leading Storm by the reins, Tom walked across the training courtyard on his way out of the palace. His sword hung from the jewelled belt around his waist, and his shield was fastened onto Storm's saddle. The stallion's hooves rang impatiently on the paving stones.

"I think Storm's as keen to set out

on our new Quest as we are," Tom remarked.

Storm blew noisily through his nose as if he were agreeing.

Silver, Elenna's grey wolf, was padding along beside his mistress. He waved his tail enthusiastically.

"You're ready, too, aren't you, boy?" Elenna asked, giving him a pat on the head. "You'll help us defeat the Ghost Beasts."

"Pick your feet up there!" Captain Harkman's shout made Tom look round. "Call yourselves soldiers?"

The young cadets Tom had trained with were jogging round and round the courtyard with packs on their backs. All of them stumbled with exhaustion, their faces streaming with sweat.

"That makes me feel bad," Tom

muttered guiltily. "I'm supposed to be with them."

"Not anymore," Elenna said with a grin.

Tom headed for the gates.

"Hey, you! Stop!" Captain Harkman strode across the courtyard, waving his riding whip. His face was red and his ginger moustache bristled. "Where do you think you're going?" he demanded. "Why didn't you report for training this morning?"

"I'm on important business for the King," Tom explained.

The Captain snorted. "Don't lie to me. Do you think I was born yesterday? Go and get your uniform on *now*, or you'll be sweeping out the barracks for the next week!"

Tom hid a smile. Digging into his pocket he brought out the scroll

King Hugo had given him the night before. He held it out to Captain Harkman. "Perhaps this will explain, sir," he said politely.

As the Captain unfastened the scroll, Tom exchanged a glance with Elenna.

Captain Harkman's gaze travelled swiftly over the paper. His eyes bulged and his face grew redder than ever. "Official business…freedom of the realm…King Hugo's seal," he spluttered.

With a final snort he shoved the scroll into Tom's hands and jogged back across the courtyard to the group of cadets, who were taking the chance to have a well-earned rest. Most of them were trying hard to suppress laughter.

"What's so funny?" Captain Harkman roared. "Get a move on!

Ten times round the courtyard, and I want to see you *run*!"

Tom and Elenna carried on towards the palace gates. Tom felt his spirits rising. There would be no more training with Captain Harkman. He was at the start of another Beast Quest. There would be challenges ahead of him, but he would do all he could to find the pieces of the amulet and bring Taladon back into the real world.

While there's blood in my veins, he thought, *I'll save my father!*

"Which way do we go?" Elenna asked. She and Tom were both riding on Storm, with Silver bounding alongside. The city walls lay behind them and the road they were on led through rolling green hills. "I'd never heard of the Forbidden Land until yesterday," she added.

"I had," Tom said, drawing Storm to a halt. "But I'm not sure where it is. That's why Wizard Aduro gave us the map." He stretched out one hand. "Map!" he called commandingly.

A grin spread over Tom's face as a patch of shimmering silver appeared, bobbing in the air in front of him. He almost felt like Wizard Aduro, able to call things up out of thin air. The silver patch was a little like the magic screen Aduro had conjured the day before to show them the story of Taladon. When Tom reached out to touch it, his fingers went right through.

"I suppose it makes sense," he murmured. "A map for finding Ghost Beasts would have to be ghostly."

Lines began to appear on the glimmering surface of the map, showing the familiar outline of Avantia, with its hills and rivers, roads and towns. But in the south and east of the kingdom a new stretch of land revealed itself.

"There!" Elenna exclaimed, peering over Tom's shoulder. "That must be the Forbidden Land – where we've got to get to."

Tom watched as letters appeared inside the region. They were small and cramped and he had to peer closely at the map to make them out.

"The Dead Valley," he said, suppressing a shiver. "That must be where we'll find the first Ghost Beast."

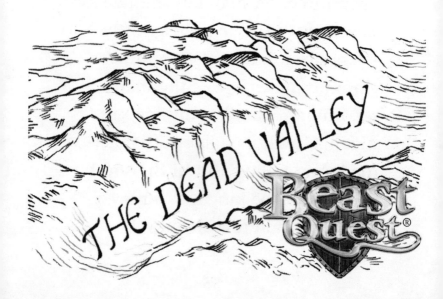

Tom rubbed the piece of horse-shoe fixed in his shield. It came from Tagus the horse-man, one of the good Beasts of Avantia, and it gave Tom extra speed while he was riding on horseback. With its help, he and Elenna travelled swiftly through the hills of Avantia, bypassing villages and crossing rivers. The sun shone, and a brisk breeze was blowing.

As the sun began to go down, Tom slowed to a normal speed again. "Well done, boy," he said to Storm, leaning forwards to pat the stallion's glossy black neck. "We've come a long way today."

"I know where we are!" Elenna cried, pointing due south to where Tom could just make out smoke rising from the huddled roof-tops of a village. "Isn't that Errinel?"

Tom nodded. He hadn't meant to pass so close to his home, but it lay near the most direct route to the Forbidden Land. To see it more clearly, he couldn't resist using the special sight from the golden helmet he had won on a previous Quest. He felt as if he were a bird, flying just above the main street, until his eyes rested on the forge where his uncle and aunt lived.

He saw his Aunt Maria come out of the house with a basket on her arm and hurry down the street towards the local market. Through the open door of the forge Tom could see his Uncle Henry beating out metal with a hammer.

"Do you want to visit?" Elenna asked. "We could spend the night with your aunt and uncle."

For a moment Tom was tempted. His home looked so welcoming; they could sleep in a proper bed, and eat one of Aunt Maria's delicious suppers. Best of all, he would see his family again.

"No," he sighed at last. "They would ask too many questions. It's best not to get distracted when we're on a Beast Quest. And how would I explain that Father is back – as a ghost?"

Tugging on the reins, he urged Storm along the road, with his back to Errinel and his face set towards the Forbidden Land.

Out there, a Ghost Beast was waiting for him.

CHAPTER FIVE

DOUBLE TAKE

The road travelled in a long loop around Errinel, then rose in a gradual slope to a gap between two hills. The land beyond the ridge fell away more steeply, with patches of dense woodland on either side of the road.

"We ought to make camp soon," Elenna suggested. "I can catch us something for supper."

"Good idea," Tom replied. "You

should be able to find something in the trees over there." He pointed to the nearest wood.

Elenna slid down off Storm's back, patted Silver a goodbye, and jogged off towards the wood, quickly disappearing among the trees.

"I'll find some grass for Storm to eat!" Tom called after her.

Elenna vanished into the thicket.

Tom got down from Storm and led him along the road. As he passed the wood he noticed several rabbits feeding. When they heard Storm's hooves, they sprang up and bounded into the undergrowth.

"Elenna's sure to catch us a good supper," Tom said to Silver.

The grey wolf let out a yelp of agreement and dashed off to catch his own food.

Tom continued down the road until he reached a spot where a spring welled up out of the ground between two jutting rocks. Lush grass grew all around the pool.

"There you go, boy," Tom said, as he unsaddled the black stallion and let him wander off to graze.

Tom splashed his face with water from the spring and took a long drink from his cupped hands. He was resting and watching Storm crop the grass when he heard footsteps behind him.

Tom turned to see Elenna striding down the road towards him. She still carried her bow, with her quiver of arrows slung over one shoulder, but Tom couldn't see any rabbits. Her mouth was set in a grim line and she was pale.

Tom sprang to his feet. "What's the matter? Where's our supper?"

Elenna threw her bow and arrows down beside the pool. "I couldn't find anything," she replied. "Not even a rabbit."

"But I saw—" Tom broke off. The look on Elenna's face stopped him saying any more. Something had obviously happened to make her unhappy, and he didn't want to upset her further.

"We ought to keep moving," Elenna snapped.

"All right." Tom's stomach was grumbling with hunger, and the sun was already low on the horizon, casting long shadows from the nearby wood across their path. They wouldn't be able to travel much further before it was dark. But he knew Elenna must have a good reason for wanting to keep going.

She'll talk to me when she's ready, Tom thought. But he couldn't ignore the prickle of unease that travelled up his spine.

"Silver went into the wood," Tom said as he picked up Storm's saddle. "He'll come if you call."

Elenna shrugged. "He'll catch us up."

Tom looked anxiously at his friend. It wasn't like her not to care whether her animal companion was with her or not. "Right, let's head for the Dead Valley," he said.

He saddled Storm and led him along the path. Elenna retrieved her bow and arrows and walked beside them; before they had gone very far, she asked, "Do you know anything about the Forbidden Land? It sounds really frightening."

Tom felt a stab of surprise. Elenna hardly ever admitted to being afraid of *anything*! "Uncle Henry used to tell me and my friends about it, in Errinel," he began, darting another glance at Elenna. "No one from Avantia is supposed to go there anymore. The legends say it used to be beautiful and prosperous, but then the evil Beasts made it their home."

Elenna shivered. "I don't think I want to go there!"

Tom could hardly believe she'd said that! "Uncle Henry told me something evil had brought the touch of death to the land," he went on. "Now it's walled off from the rest of Avantia. We'll have to—"

"Tom! Tom!"

A familiar voice behind him froze
Tom in his tracks. He turned, his
heart almost stopping as he saw
Elenna racing down the path
towards him.

But Elenna's right beside me! Tom
whirled back to glance at his friend,
who had stopped when he did. Then
he turned to the other Elenna. There
were two of them!

CHAPTER SIX

THE SOUND OF EVIL

Tom gripped his sword and drew
it out of its sheath. Now he
remembered what Wizard Aduro had
told him: Nixa the Ghost Beast was a
shape-shifter! She could appear in
any form she wanted.

I can't believe I've been so stupid!
he thought. *Elenna isn't scared of
Quests…and she never fails at hunting.*

And she would definitely never leave Silver behind!

"You're not Elenna!" he shouted at the figure by his side. His hand trembled with the struggle of aiming his sword at someone who looked

like his friend. "You're Nixa the death-bringer!"

"No!" The Elenna he had accused stepped back, raising her hands to protect herself. Her eyes were wide with terror and her face twisted in an ugly grimace. "You've got it wrong, Tom! I'm the real Elenna...*she's* Nixa!"

"Tom!" the other Elenna called out, pounding even faster down the path to reach them. "Defeat her now! She's Nixa!"

Tom looked from one to the other, his sword stretched out in front of him. His hand shook with the agony of deciding. He *had* to confront the Beast, but he couldn't risk hurting Elenna – he needed to be absolutely certain which was the real one.

"I can't be sure..." he whispered.

The Elenna at Tom's side stepped forwards and grabbed the other Elenna as she reached them. She whirled her around until Tom wasn't sure anymore which was which. They were both dressed in the same clothes, with the same untidy hair and the same smudge of dirt across their foreheads. They carried the same bows and arrows.

I don't know! screamed a voice inside Tom's head.

Then he heard furious yelps coming from the direction of the wood. Silver was charging across the grass, his strong legs pumping. Reaching the road, he hurled himself at the Elenna nearest Tom, all the hairs on his back bristling with anger.

"Clever boy!" Tom exclaimed. "The Ghost Beast can't fool you!"

The fake Elenna staggered back as Silver crashed into her. "Get off, you flea-bitten animal!" she cried.

Her shape flickered and changed into the form of the beautiful woman in scarlet silk that Tom had seen on Aduro's magical screen. Silver passed right through her and landed on the path beyond with a whimper of sheer astonishment.

Gripping his sword, Tom faced Nixa. She had two options for attacking him, he realised. When she was flesh and blood, she was strong but could be injured, whereas in her ghostly form no one could touch her.

But I have to try, he thought.

Tom swung his sword wildly – too wildly. The tip caught on a boulder, dragging across the surface of the stone with a harsh, grating sound.

A deep shudder passed through Nixa. Her face set into a grimace of fear and loathing. Tom stared as slime broke out all over her body, her eyes multiplied and she became the tentacled monster that had attacked his father.

Silver crouched beside the Beast, growling, while Storm let out a startled whinny and backed rapidly away.

Nixa shrank from them, then turned and fled down the road.

"What's happening?" Elenna asked, coming to stand beside Tom. "What's the matter with her?"

"It must have been the *sound*," Tom replied, watching the space where Nixa had been. "She hated the noise my sword made on the rock. Now I know how to defeat her!"

A blue light shone out behind him, casting his and Elenna's shadows ahead of them.

Tom whirled round. A man stood in the shimmering light: his father, Taladon. He still looked weak and ghostly.

Tom gasped with surprise. He hadn't expected to see his father again until his Quest was completed.

"You're lucky to be alive," Taladon said. "You shouldn't get too close to Nixa."

"But she ran before we could even fight," Tom replied. "How can I defeat her if I mustn't get close to her?"

"She has a weapon you don't know about yet. I'm here to warn you: be careful of her voice," his father told him.

"You said her voice was beautiful," Elenna said, frowning. "How can it be dangerous?"

"Beautiful and deadly," said Taladon. "It feels like a dagger of ice, piercing your ears and your heart. Few who hear it have lived. Take care, Tom. If you let Nixa get too close to you, she will use her voice. If your sword hadn't scraped the boulder, you could all be dead by now. Nixa is a Beast who lives and dies through heart-wrenching sounds…"

Taladon's voice began to fade away, and the shimmering blue light dimmed.

"Wait!" Tom exclaimed. "I want to ask—"

But Taladon had vanished.

Tom turned to Elenna. "I wanted to know how my father managed to defeat Nixa."

"We'll work something out ourselves," Elenna assured him. "We always do."

Silver, who had stayed crouched on the ground while Taladon was speaking, got up, gave himself a shake, and trotted over to Elenna. She ruffled his fur and he pressed close to her side.

Tom walked over to where Storm was standing, and patted the stallion's neck. "Come on, boy. We've got to find Nixa now, and get the piece of the amulet before she does any more harm."

Tom swung himself onto Storm's saddle and held out a hand to help Elenna up behind him.

"Nixa shouldn't give us too much trouble, now we know what frightens her," Elenna said, as they set off along the road once more.

"I'm not so sure," Tom said. An unpleasant thought sent shivers of apprehension down his spine. "She ran away from the noise, but what was she doing here in the first place? The Ghost Beasts are supposed to stay in the Forbidden Land – but Nixa dared to come out and meet us right here, in the middle of Avantia. What else will she dare to do?"

CHAPTER SEVEN

A TOUCH OF MAGIC

"Look! Over there!" Tom reined in Storm as he and Elenna emerged from a belt of trees. Ahead of them lay a high grey wall, stretching far into the distance and barring their way. "That must be the Forbidden Land."

"How are we going to get in?" Elenna asked, peering over Tom's shoulder. "We'll never be able to climb that."

"There must be a way," Tom said, urging Storm forwards again.

As they drew closer, Tom could see that he was right. The road led up to an arched opening in the wall. Two heavy wooden gates, studded with brass nails, blocked their path.

Tom jumped down from his horse and pushed at the gates. To his surprise, they swung open easily, and he, Elenna and the animals passed through them.

Tom pushed the gates closed again and looked around. Behind him lay the rich fields and woods of Avantia, but all the land on this side of the wall was grey and dead. There was no movement and no sound except for the whistling of the wind. A grey haze covered the sky.

"I can't believe we're still in Avantia," Elenna said with a shiver.

"The Ghost Beasts have made it like this," said Tom, clenching his fists. Now that he saw the Forbidden Land for himself, he was even more determined to fight the Beasts. No part of Avantia should be so desolate!

The road wound ahead through stony hills. Tom climbed back onto Storm and they pressed forwards.

"This should take us to the Dead Valley," he said, remembering what he had seen on Wizard Aduro's magic map. "That's where we'll find Nixa."

They travelled under the blank grey sky, which was getting darker by the minute. Storm's hooves threw up clouds of dust, stinging Tom and Elenna's eyes, and making them cough. Silver padded along with his head down and his tongue lolling.

The road began to climb steeply until it reached a rocky plateau. Huddled shapes were scattered here and there across the flat surface. Silver bounded up to the nearest one and sniffed at it. Then he raised his head and let out a mournful howl.

"Something's wrong!" Elenna's voice was full of anxiety.

Tom guided Storm over. Horror crept over him as he realised that the shape was the body of a man, lying face down with his arms wrapped round his head as if he were trying to protect himself. He didn't look like a citizen of Avantia – his skin was as grey as the land around them.

These people must live in the Forbidden Land, Tom thought. Aduro hadn't told him that anyone survived here.

"I think he's dead," Elenna whispered.

Silver looked up, whining miserably, and Storm shied away, refusing to come any closer.

Tom leant forwards to pat the stallion's neck. "Steady, boy. We need to find out what happened, and then we'll be on our way."

He slid down from the saddle and Elenna followed. As he bent over the body, Tom could see that Elenna was right: the man was dead.

"Nixa must be close," he murmured. "This man hasn't been dead for long. But what's he doing here, anyway? No one from Avantia should set foot in the Forbidden Land."

"Look – blood." Elenna was

pointing to dark, sticky pools on either side of the man's head.

"He bled from the ears!" An icy shiver ran down Tom's spine.

"Nixa must have used her voice," Elenna said nervously.

Looking round, Tom could now see that the other shapes were bodies too, all of them with dusty, grey skin. They seemed to form a trail leading across the plateau. Perhaps they were travellers who had mistakenly wandered into this deadly region.

"At least it should be easy to track Nixa down," Tom said grimly.

They mounted Storm again and set off, following the trail of bodies. All the men and women seemed to have tried to cover their ears. They all had the tell-tale pools of blood beside their head. Two of the bodies were dogs, who had died with their legs stretched out, as if they had been trying to leap on Nixa.

The sight of the bodies only made Tom more determined to defeat the Beast. *Somehow I have to stop her!* he thought.

At last, the trail of bodies led them to a gaping hole in the rocky hillside. It was a tunnel, leading into the hill; Tom caught a glimpse of wooden posts holding up its roof.

"This must be an old mine," he said.

"Nixa might be in there," Elenna suggested. "It would be a good hiding-place."

"Let's check." Tom stretched out his hand. "Map!"

At once the ghostly map shimmered in front of Tom. A picture of the mine formed on its shining surface, with a tiny picture of Nixa hovering over it.

"I think you could be right," Tom said to Elenna, banishing the map again with a wave of his hand. "She's in there somewhere."

Tom tried to suppress the chill that tingled through him. "There'll be echoes in the mine," he went on. "Nixa's voice will be even louder. We need something to protect our ears."

Elenna jumped down from Storm and cautiously approached the mine's entrance. Tom dismounted, summoning all the magical strength of heart that he could gain from the golden chainmail. But even with its power, he wasn't sure he could force his feet to carry him into the mine where Nixa was lurking. If he and Elenna heard the Ghost Beast's evil voice, they would be facing certain death.

"But I have to try," he muttered to himself. "My father is depending on me."

Resolutely he turned towards the gaping entrance. But before he could step forwards, a swirling blue light sprang up between him and the dark hole. This time, it was the form of Wizard Aduro that took shape.

"Well done, Tom." The wizard's voice sounded clearly inside Tom's head. "No one in Avantia will ever doubt your courage. But a little magic never did any harm."

He raised his hands, and blue light streamed from his fingertips. It formed into tendrils that touched Tom and Elenna on both ears.

Tom started as he saw Elenna's lips move, but he couldn't hear a thing!

"I have enchanted your ears," Aduro explained, his voice sounding inside Tom's head. "You will be protected for a little while. But inside the mines my magic is weak. Once you go in there, it will start to fade. You do not have long, so you must hurry!"

Tom and Elenna exchanged a glance and nodded vigorously.

"Good luck!" Aduro said as the blue light began to fade.

When the wizard vanished, Tom turned to Storm and unslung his shield from his saddle. "Wait here, boy." It felt strange to speak and not hear the sound of his own voice. "We'll be back soon."

Elenna crouched beside Silver, stroking the thick fur on his neck. Tom couldn't hear what she was saying to the wolf, but a moment later she straightened up and gestured towards the entrance of the mine.

Tom drew his sword, and led the way into the darkness.

CHAPTER EIGHT

INTO THE CAVE

The light from the entrance died away behind Tom and Elenna as they ventured cautiously along the tunnel. Tom couldn't see anything. He guided himself by touching the wall with his free hand. He could feel Elenna close behind him, her hand on his shoulder.

Before they had gone very far, Tom began to feel a tingling in his feet, and in the fingers that touched the tunnel wall. The walls and floor were vibrating!

"Nixa must be using her voice against us," he said, before he remembered that Elenna couldn't hear him. *But it's not going to work*, he thought. *We're much smarter than she is!*

Eventually, Tom thought he could make out the tunnel stretching in front of him. A faint light trickled in from somewhere up ahead. As he and Elenna walked forwards the light grew stronger, until they came out into a wide open space. Thin shafts of weak light shone down from gaps and crevices.

Stalactites hung from the roof of the cave, while stalagmites grew up from the floor. Tom thought they looked like rows of huge, misshapen teeth.

Elenna prodded Tom sharply in the

back and pointed to the other side of the cave. Tom braced himself as he caught a glimpse of a monstrous creature weaving its way in and out of the stalagmites. He recognised the coiling tentacles and skin dripping with slime.

Nixa!

Tom could see the Ghost Beast's mouth moving. He knew that she was using her deadly voice, yet he couldn't hear a thing. With Elenna just behind him, he darted from one stalagmite to the next, trying to stay hidden as he made his way towards the Beast.

But Nixa spotted them. Her clumps of eyes bulged with rage.

She knows we can't hear her, Tom thought.

Nixa's huge mouth gaped wide, as if she were letting out a shriek. A fierce wind whipped through the cave; Tom and Elenna grabbed the nearest stalagmite so the blast wouldn't sweep them away.

The wind ripped chunks of rock from the stalactites and stalagmites, and sent them hurtling towards Tom and Elenna. Tom grabbed his friend and dived for cover behind the stalagmite.

"Coward!" he yelled; he couldn't hear himself, but he knew Nixa would hear him. "Come closer and fight me!"

Tom managed to unsling his shield in time to ward off the first of the rocks. *This is so strange*, he thought. He could feel the thump of the rocks as they hit his shield and bounced off, and he could see them crashing to the cave floor, but he couldn't hear a sound. *It's like a dream, as if it isn't really happening.*

As he crouched, Tom could feel the vibrations in the cave floor and the stalagmite growing stronger. *Either Nixa's getting louder – or Aduro's magic is starting to fail*, he thought.

Tom knew he had no time to waste. Springing up, he charged straight at Nixa, whirling his sword above his head.

Just as he reached the monster, Nixa swiftly changed her shape. She became the beautiful woman dressed in scarlet robes. But Tom would not be deterred. "For Avantia!" he yelled, even though he couldn't hear himself. He struck at Nixa with all his strength, but passed right through her, just as he had passed through Taladon back at the palace. She'd changed into her ghostly form.

Tom gritted his teeth with fury. *We'll have to outwit her, not outfight her,* he realised.

He spun round. Nixa stood in front of him, her head thrown back as she laughed. In one hand she held up a broken piece of silver decorated with a sliver of blue enamel.

Tom tensed as he recognised part of the Amulet of Avantia. If he could get it, he would be one step closer to saving his father.

While there's blood in my veins, he vowed, *I will not fail!*

CHAPTER NINE

STRENGTH OF THE SWORD

Tom remembered how Nixa had run
away when he scraped his sword
against the rock by the side of the
road. *That's it!* he realised. *We have to
use sound to defeat her!*

Darting to the nearby wall of the
cave, Tom scraped his sword across it.
Though he couldn't hear the noise,
he saw sparks flying out and chips of

rock scattering everywhere.

Nixa's beautiful face took on a look of horror. Her mouth gaped wide, and Tom felt the vibrations of her screams drilling at his ears.

They hadn't got long before Aduro's protection wore off!

He stepped forwards to face Nixa again. The Ghost Beast, her eyes wild with fear, swept towards Tom and straight through him. She was heading for the tunnel from which Tom and Elenna had entered the cave.

We can't let her escape! Tom thought, as he took off after her.

Elenna was standing in Nixa's way. She gripped one of her arrows and drew it down the side of one of the stalagmites.

"Well done, Elenna!" Tom yelled.

His friend started, alarmed, as if she'd heard something. But Tom couldn't waste time worrying about the enchantment fading. At the sound from Elenna's arrow, Nixa had turned back and was rushing straight for him.

Tom drew his sword across the stone floor of the cave, and Nixa halted once again. Trapped between Tom and Elenna, she was starting to panic. Her mouth gaped as she kept on screaming.

This isn't working, Tom thought, as he scraped his sword again. *She can't get away, but I can't defeat her like this.*

The vibrations in the cave floor were growing stronger and it was hard for Tom to keep his balance. His ears were starting to hum with a dull pain; across the cave he saw Elenna shaking her head uncomfortably, as if she could feel it too. Wizard Aduro's enchantment was fading. Soon they would be forced to listen to Nixa's deadly voice.

"I've got to do something!" Tom exclaimed aloud, trying to shut out Nixa's screams. "It's now or never!"

Tom summoned the power of his magical boots and leapt at Nixa. His confidence surged back as he felt the magical golden armour boosting him high into the air. As he came down, he scraped his sword against the wall of the cave, making an ear-splitting noise. The Ghost Beast backed away from the sound, but Tom landed right beside her, passing through the outer folds of her scarlet robes with the force of his landing.

Tom made a grab for the piece of amulet. Nixa snatched it away from him, and as Tom reached for it again, she shifted into the form of the many-eyed monster dripping with slime. One set of tentacles lashed around Tom's waist, and with another tentacle she held the silver fragment high out of Tom's reach.

Struggling against Nixa's fierce grip, Tom managed to bend over and drag his sword across the rocky cave floor.

Nixa's tentacles uncoiled and she threw Tom against the wall of the cave. He slumped to the ground, his vision blurred and the breath driven

out of him. When he could get up,
he saw Elenna with her bow out,
firing arrow after arrow into Nixa's
slimy body.

The Ghost Beast bellowed in rage as
she tugged the shafts out and flung
them aside. The low hum in Tom's
ears grew louder, and pain stabbed
sharply into his head. Nixa was
charging across the cave, straight at
Elenna.

No! Scrambling to his feet, Tom
dropped his shield and leapt upon
Nixa. He knew he had to use the
noise of his sword to destroy her,
before all the enchantment was gone.
He grabbed one of her tentacles,
digging his fingers into the slippery
surface, and wrenched her round to
face him. At the same moment he
scraped his sword down the nearest

stalagmite – close enough to Nixa for the sound to terrify her.

Nixa let out a furious shriek. The pain of her voice made Tom let go of her tentacle, and dropping his sword, he clapped his hands over his ears. He felt as if daggers were stabbing deep into his head.

Elenna had fallen to her knees. She was trying to shut the sound out too, her arms wrapped around her head. She exchanged an agonised glance with Tom.

In a daze of pain, Tom grabbed his sword again and dragged it across the floor one last time. The Ghost Beast's scream was abruptly cut off. Her monstrous body seemed to swell, then exploded in a shower of slimy fragments. They spattered over the cave walls and floor, letting out a foul smell.

The piece of amulet fell to the ground. Tom ran over and picked it up, holding it over his head in triumph.

Elenna grinned delightedly. "You did it! You've got the first piece!" she exclaimed. "That was amazing!"

Tom laughed. It was good to hear his friend's voice again. "We did it together," he said.

Tom fitted his sword into its sheath and rubbed the scrap of amulet on his tunic to get rid of Nixa's slime. It shone as it reflected the fading light above them.

Meanwhile, Elenna crossed the cave to retrieve the arrows she had shot at Nixa. "They're all covered in slime," she said. "That Beast was disgusting!"

As Tom waited for her, he realised that a shimmering blue light was growing behind him. He spun round to see his father smiling at him.

"Well done, both of you," said Taladon. "Tom, you make me proud."

Tom held up the fragment of the amulet. "Look, Father, I rescued the first piece."

Taladon nodded. "So I see. I can feel my strength beginning to return already. I know I won't be a ghost for ever – not with you to help me." Tom could see that his father's shape already looked stronger, as if life was flowing back into him.

Tom's heart swelled with pride, but at the same time a faint uneasiness touched him like icy fingers. *I feel weak,* he thought. *What's wrong with me?*

Elenna hurried to join Tom and his father, a bunch of arrows in her hand. "What happens now?" she asked.

"You must find the next piece of the amulet," Taladon told them. Already his ghostly form was starting to fade. "It's in the keeping of Equinus the spirit horse."

"We won't fail you!" Tom called out as his father vanished.

With Elenna beside him, he headed
for the mouth of the cave and into
the tunnel. This time they pushed
on quickly through the darkness,
until they could see the grey light of
the Forbidden Land shining dimly
ahead of them.

Tom called on his magic powers to leap forwards, eager to see Storm and Silver again. But somehow he lost his balance as he took off, and tumbled to his knees against the tunnel wall.

"Are you hurt?" Elenna asked anxiously. "Tom? What's wrong?"

Tom shook his head. For a moment the breath had been driven out of his body. "I'm fine, he gasped. "I just took off badly, that's all."

But I still feel weak, he thought to himself. *Something's wrong…*

He tried to push his suspicions out of his mind, but he couldn't stop wondering why he had failed to summon enough power for his leap.

He led the way out of the tunnel. This wasn't the time to start worrying. They had to go once more into the Forbidden Land, and track down Equinus the spirit horse, wherever he might be.

Whatever happens, Tom told himself, *I'll bring my father back to his human form!* Another Quest was waiting for them.

Here's a sneak preview of Tom's
next exciting adventure!

Meet

EQUINUS
THE
SPIRIT HORSE

Only Tom can defeat the
Ghost Beasts and save his father...

PROLOGUE

"Now it's your turn to give me a dare!" Jak told his friend Flint.

The boys were playing on the edge of their village. The sun had almost set over Errinel and heavy shadows were creeping across the ground. The sky was the colour of a deep purple bruise, but the approaching darkness just made their game of dare even better. Flint looked around and Jak saw his eyes light up as he pointed towards some trees in a nearby field.

"Dare you to pinch an apple from Farmer Grindall's orchard," said Flint.

"No problem!" Jak vaulted over a wooden fence, strolled into the orchard and climbed up the tallest apple tree. He'd show Flint he wasn't scared – even though grumpy old Farmer Grindall would chase him with a stick if he saw him.

As he reached the top branch, he had a good view of the road that led away from the village and ran alongside the boundary of Avantia, King Hugo's realm. It was marked by a high forbidding wall with an old iron gate, but even from his position in the tree, Jak couldn't see over it. Beyond the wall was the Forbidden Land. Jak knew that no one ever went near there. The other villagers wouldn't even talk about it. But looking at the black sinister wall gave him an idea for the best dare ever!

He plucked an apple, swung down from the tree and jumped back over the fence.

"You win that one," admitted Flint, as Jak tossed him the apple.

"Now here's your next dare," said Jak. "It's so frightening I bet you won't do it."

"Nothing's too frightening for me!" Flint said confidently.

"I dare you to go into the Forbidden Land!" challenged Jak. He folded his arms, sure that his friend would admit defeat. *I wonder which forfeit I should give him*, he thought.

But Flint didn't say a word. Instead, he strode down the road to the gate in the wall.

Jak ran after him, his heart beating hard. "You don't have to do it," he called. "It was just a joke."

"I never say no to a dare," said Flint, and he grasped the ironwork and began to climb.

"Then I'm coming with you."

The gate was rusty and felt unstable beneath Jak's grip as he scrambled up it. He climbed on. He couldn't let his friend go alone.

The boys were soon sitting astride the gate, staring in amazement at the sight before them. The Forbidden Land was grey as far as the eye could see. The ground was covered with a thick layer of dust and the only trees that grew nearby were blackened and gnarled.

"It's horrible!" Flint said with a gasp.

"Everything is so dead looking," murmured Jak in reply.

They slid to the ground of the Forbidden Land and walked slowly away from the gate. Their boots left deep prints in the ash-like powder. Jak saw his friend shiver.

"We've done the dare," Flint said. His voice sounded odd and flat in this strange place and the gate suddenly seemed a long way away. "Let's get back."

Jak nodded but suddenly spotted something on the horizon. "What's that?"

Flint followed his gaze. "It looks like a dust cloud." His face suddenly looked worried and he glanced down at his feet. "Can you feel the ground?"

Jak could. The grey earth beneath their feet was vibrating and sending shudders up their legs.

"Something's coming," he whispered. The boys stood transfixed as the cloud of dust got nearer, and as the vibrations coming from the ground became stronger.

"It's a horse!" Flint exclaimed, peering into the distance. "And it's big."

Jak looked hard. His friend was right. He could just make out a glint of hooves and he realised that the hoofbeats must be causing the vibrations. He caught a glimpse of a man sitting tall in the saddle. "I wonder who the rider is," he said as the horse got closer. "No, wait…"

With rising horror, he saw that the man's body was joined to the horse. It was some kind of Beast – part man, part horse. But the Beasts didn't exist, did they? They were just made-up stories of Avantia that Jak repeated when he wanted to scare his little brother.

The Beast suddenly became transparent and Jak felt his jaw drop open in shock.

"I can see right through him." Flint swallowed nervously. "It's a ghost. And it's coming straight for us!"

Jak and Flint dashed for the gate, their feet churning up the grey dust. The Beast was getting closer but the boys were fast runners. *We're going to make it*, Jak thought with relief. But just as they got to the wall, Flint tripped and fell sprawling into the dust.

Jak quickly helped him stand but above their heads came an almighty roar. The friends looked up. The Beast, solid once again, was on top of them and rearing up on its hind legs ready to crush them. Jak gazed at the Beast and saw an expression of terrible delight etched onto his skeleton-like face.

The boys were paralysed with fear and screamed as the terrifying Beast lunged down. Jak felt an icy cold sweep over his whole body and gasped as he realised that the Beast had turned ghostly again and somehow passed straight through him.

Tears of despair trickled down Jak's face as he felt something being torn from him. He forced himself to look at Flint. His friend stood pale and expressionless.

With his last thought, Jak knew what had happened to them both. The Beasts were real, after all. And this one might not have crushed them, but he had done something far worse. He had taken their life force.

Follow this Quest to the end in EQUINUS THE SPIRIT HORSE.

Win an exclusive
Beast Quest T-shirt and goody bag!

Tom has battled many fearsome Beasts and we want to know
which one is your favourite! Send us a drawing or painting of
your favourite Beast and tell us in 30 words why you think
it's the best.

Each month we will select **three** winners to receive
a Beast Quest T-shirt and goody bag!

Send your entry on a postcard to
BEAST QUEST COMPETITION
Orchard Books, 338 Euston Road, London NW1 3BH.

Australian readers should email:
childrens.books@hachette.com.au

New Zealand readers should write to:
Beast Quest Competition, PO Box 3255, Shortland St,
Auckland 1140, NZ or email: childrensbooks@hachette.co.nz

**Don't forget to include your name and address.
Only one entry per child.**

Good luck!

Fight the Beasts,
Fear the Magic

www.beastquest.co.uk

Have you checked out the Beast Quest website?
It's the place to go for games, downloads, activities,
sneak previews and lots of fun!

You can read all about your favourite beasts,
download free screensavers and desktop wallpapers
for your computer, and even challenge your friends
to a Beast Tournament.

Sign up to the newsletter at www.beastquest.co.uk
to receive exclusive extra content and the
opportunity to enter special members-only
competitions. We'll send you up-to-date info on all
the Beast Quest books, including the next exciting
series which features four brand-new Beasts!

FREE COLLECTOR CARDS INSIDE!

Series 1
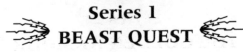
BEAST QUEST

An evil wizard has enchanted the Beasts that guard
Avantia. Is Tom the hero who can free them?

978 1 84616 483 5

978 1 84616 482 8

978 1 84616 484 2

978 1 84616 486 6

978 1 84616 485 9

978 1 84616 487 3

978 1 84616 951 9

SPECIAL BUMPER EDITION!

Can Tom save the baby
dragons from Malvel's
evil plans?

Series 2
THE GOLDEN ARMOUR

Tom must find the pieces of the magical golden armour.
But they are guarded by six terrifying Beasts!

978 1 84616 988 5

978 1 84616 989 2

978 1 84616 990 8

978 1 84616 991 5

978 1 84616 992 2

978 1 84616 993 9

978 1 84616 994 6

SPECIAL BUMPER EDITION!

Will Tom find Spiros
in time to save his
aunt and uncle?

Series 3
THE DARK REALM

To rescue the good Beasts, Tom must brave the
terrifying Dark Realm and six terrible new Beasts...

978 1 84616 997 7

978 1 84616 998 4

978 1 40830 000 8

978 1 40830 001 5

978 1 40830 002 2

978 1 40830 003 9

978 1 40830 382 5

Arax has stolen
Aduro's soul – and
now he wants Tom's...

All books priced at £4.99.
Special bumper editions priced at £5.99.

Orchard Books are available from all good bookshops, or can
be ordered from our website: www.orchardbooks.co.uk,
or telephone 01235 827702, or fax 01235 8227703.